For Lauren, Dusty, and Ruby.

Library of Congress Cataloging-in-Publication Data available.

ISBN 978-1-4521-8270-4

Manufactured in China.

Design by Jennifer Tolo Pierce.
Typeset in Acre.
The illustrations in this book were made with
pencil and colored pencil.

10 9 8 7 6 5 4 3 2 1

Chronicle Books LLC
680 Second Street
San Francisco, California 94107

Chronicle Books—we see things differently.
Become part of our community at
www.chroniclekids.com.

HAVE YOU EVER SEEN A FLOWER?

BY SHAWN HARRIS

chronicle books · san francisco

Have you ever seen a flower?

I mean *really* . . .

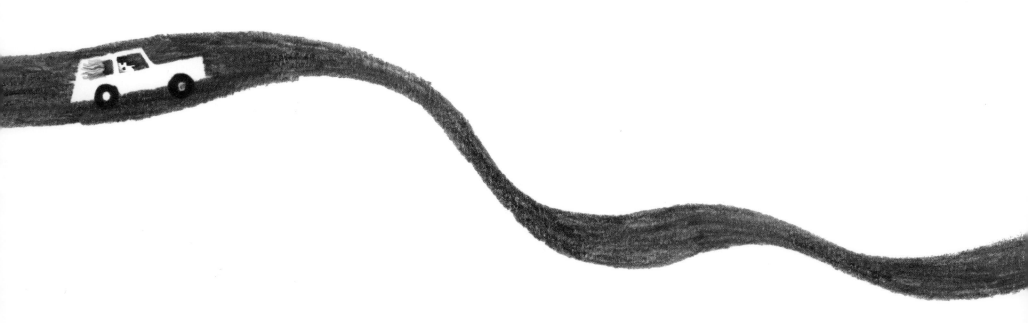

seen a flower?

I mean way down in the clover

with your face down in a flower?

Have you ever
seen a flower
using nothing
but your nose?

Breathe deep . . .

what do you see?

A fancy lady?

Dancing babies at the royal jelly jubilee?

Have you ever seen
a flower so deep
        you had to shout

HELLO

and listen for an echo
        just to know
            how deep it goes?

And did you wonder, if you wandered
down between its golden columns
and into its corridors,

who you might meet?

Maybe a tiny queen?

Have you ever felt a flower?

Do a flower petal's veins

feel like the veins beneath your skin?

Have you ever pricked your finger

or fallen on your knee

and seen the brilliant color of your life?

Life
is
inside
you.

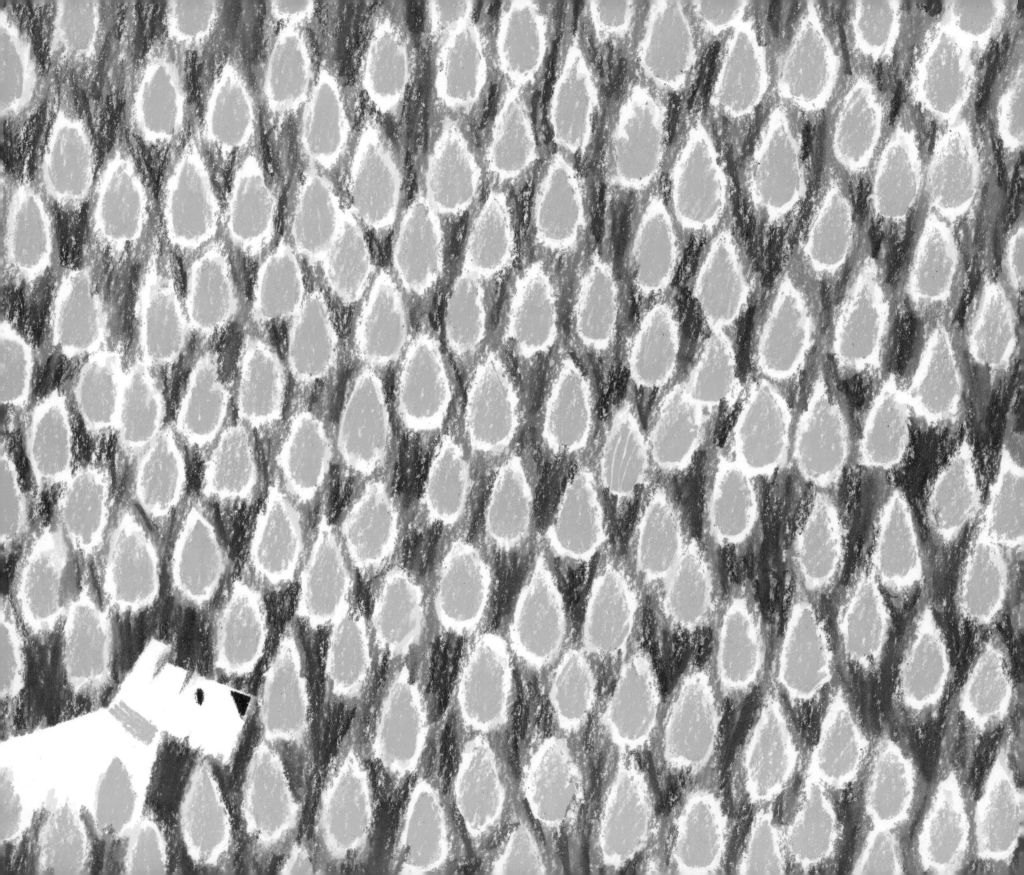

Now put your hands on your belly

and say, "This is my stem."

Now sip a drip of water, and stand very still.

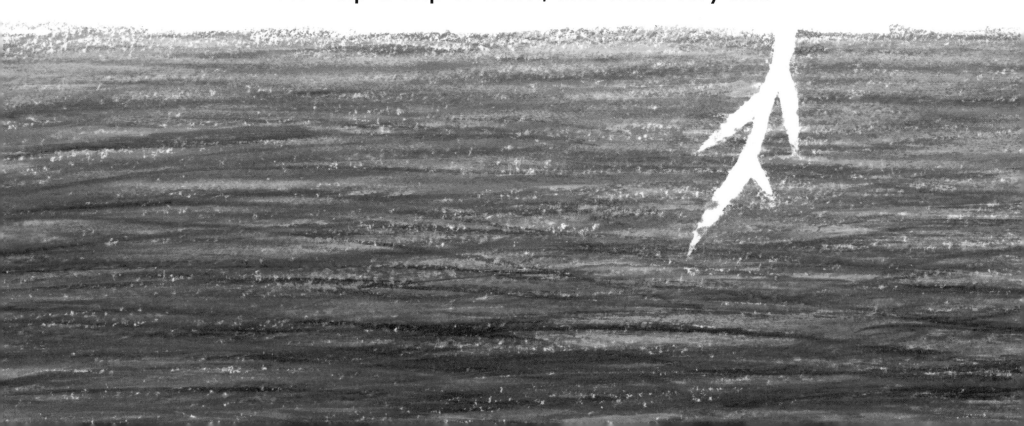

Feel it slip and trickle all the way down to your roots.

Do you feel yourself growing?

Do you feel yourself stretching toward the sun,

ready to burst . . .

and bloom?

Have you ever been a flower?

I mean *really* been a flower?

And if you were . . .   would you remember?

Try

and

see.